For Annie,
Love you always,
Mommy

To My Mother,
She always believed in me.
N.M.

~ Special Thanks ~
To my Family–
for their unceasing encouragement, love and support
and to God, Psalm 145

Text & Illustrations Copyright © 2013 J. Eileen Arness
Black & White Illustrations Copyright © 2013 Nancy Mullikin
Graphic Design by Zack Mullikin
For information please write:
J. Eileen Arness/Editor
P.O. Box 40507
St. Petersburg, FL 33743

ISBN 978-0-9894336-0-0

A Tale of
Moon Cheese

Roger was a mouse who lived in a deli,
Where they had lots of cheeses, some sweet and some smelly.

He lived with his family in a den by the door,
Just across from the cheese case, in a hole on the floor.

Roger loved cheese like all little mice should,
But his was a passion that few understood.

He knew them by name—Swiss, Cheddar and Gruyere,
But the one he sought most lived up in the air.

He saw it one night looking up at the sky,
It was BIG, glowing bright, like a warm custard pie.

He was sure it was cheese - it was creamy and bumpy,
Golden and round and not too lumpy.

It glowed like Smoked Cheddar, had cracks like a Bleu,
And would taste even better! Oh, he just KNEW!

"Papa," asked Roger one crisp autumn night,
"What's the name of that cheese in the sky glowing bright?"

Papa smiled and said with a twinkle in his eye,
"It's called the Moon, up there in the sky."

Now, Papa knew Roger was a bit like himself,
And would probably seek "Moon Cheese" up on the shelf.

For the deli had cheeses and pickles and eggs,
Ham and fresh bread- even root beer in kegs.

But "Moon Cheese"? No, Papa had never seen that,
Not in all of his years, but kept it under his hat.

For children need dreams, and who was to say,
For Roger might find "Moon Cheese" some day.

"Run along," said Papa, "but be back before dawn,
Flynn and Fannie are waiting, and the cat's on the lawn."

He caught up with his siblings, being one of three.
He couldn't wait to tell them what he did see.

"You've got to come see it!" he did implore,
"Outside of the window, right by the door!"

"Later!" Flynn mumbled, stuffing his cheeks.
"Maybe tomorrow?" Fannie said with a squeak.

Soon it was late and they had to return,
For the cat had come in and was sniffing the churn.

As they passed the front window, Roger looked 'round about.
The Sun began gleaming and the Moon wasn't out.

With a sigh he jumped down and ran into the lair,
Mama gave him a hug and Papa rumpled his hair.

Papa looked down at his children all three,
And said "Come by the fire and sit next to me."

Then he put on his glasses and sipped his tea,
And gathered his mouse-lings, who sat by his knee.

"I have a story to tell you of old mousy lore,
And cheese you might find someday out in the store."

Three little faces looked up in wonder,
As his story began, to the rumble of thunder.

"An old legend says, on the darkest of nights,
The Moon comes to Earth, so we have a bite."

"The texture so tender, it melts like a Brie,
The sweetness and splendor, like salt in the sea."

"And just when you think it's all been consumed,
The Moon appears again like a flower that's bloomed."

The three little ones started stretching and yawning,
Most assuredly it was bedtime for the day was past dawning.

"Come children," said Mama smiling sweet,
"Kiss your Papa goodnight and get under the sheet."

So they all said their prayers and jumped right into bed,
And Mama planted a kiss on each little head.

"Tomorrow would come," Roger contentedly pondered,
"And then I will show them..."– his mind drifted and wandered.

He dreamed the sweet dreams only little mice know,
Of Moonbeams and how cheese in the candlelight glows.

A rumble of thunder jolted Roger awake.
A storm was coming, there could be no mistake.

It rained the next night, so the Moon wasn't there,
Roger couldn't help but sit by the window and stare.

"C'mon!" yelled Flynn, "let's go get some food!"
"Yeah!" squeaked Fannie, "it might lighten your mood!"

With a sigh Roger leaped down off of the sill,
And scampered into the shop to eat his fill.

The children ran into the Deli to plunder,
And out in the dark night was a loud CLAP of thunder.

"Roger!" yelled Flynn from atop a large cheese,
"Did you say something, or was that a sneeze?"

"A sneeze," replied Roger, "but your timing's uncanny,
I was just about to ask, have you seen Fannie?"

Looking around through the flashes of lightning,
They spotted Fannie looking at something quite frightening.

The boys scampered over as quiet as could be,
Then crept up beside her so they too could see-

Wide –eyed, mouth agape, she thought she would swoon,
"Roger," she said, "could that be the Moon?"

The three gazed upon a wondrous new cheese,
So luminous and white, it made them all freeze.

But Roger stepped closer, he sniffed, then he stared,
"I don't know Fannie, but you shouldn't be scared."

"I'm not scared!" replied Fannie looking a bit hurt,
"It just smells to me, well, a lot like dessert."

Flynn crept up with the greatest of stealth-
"Maybe the Moon was upset and not feeling itself,
So it came here to rest on the top of this shelf."

"Maybe," said Roger, "though it could be the rain,
I know I'd come in if I heard thunder again."

"Me, too," said Fannie, "but the sky is pitch black,
And with the cat out roaming, we should really get back."

So the three little mice scampered back to the den,
Where Mama and Papa were waiting for them.

They popped in the door and jumped all around,
Excitedly telling of what they had found.

"Please little ones! All this squeaking and hopping!
You're going to fall down, 'cause your Mother's been mopping!"

"Come settle down and tell me each one,
What did you find that has you so undone?"

"The Moon! The Moon! It's up in the case!"
Squeaked Roger and Flynn with a smile on their face.

"Papa," said Fannie, "I disagree,
It smelled much more like a sweetie to me."

Papa thought to himself, *"could it really be true?"*
The story was just that for all that he knew.

"Come Mama, come children, we'll go see what's there,
If the Moon has come down for us all to share."

Mama grabbed her shawl and Papa his hat,
And they scampered out quickly, avoiding the cat.

The Moon was still missing from the sky up above,
Could this really be "Moon Cheese" they all had dreamed of?

They jumped in the case, while gazing in awe,
At the shining spectre of that which they saw.

It truly was big, so soft and glowing,
And white on top, like it had been snowing.

Papa crept closer, he sniffed and then he twitched–
Could this be "Moon Cheese" that had them bewitched?

Papa nibbled the cheese, closed his eyes with delight,
So sweet and delicious, so creamy and light!

"Dear children, your discovery is not what it seems,
It's called a *cheesecake* and it's better than dreams."

"Come join me," said Papa, "eat to your hearts content,
This cheesecake, so delectable, is heaven sent!"

"But Papa," said Roger a little dismayed,
"Are you sure it's not 'Moon Cheese'?" he tried to persuade.

Just then the light shifted and to eliminate doubt,
The clouds had been lifted and the Moon had come out!

"Look there," said Mama, "the Moon's up in the sky–
It can't be down here AND up there on high."

"I guess not," said Roger, his spirits brightening,
He then had a thought that struck him like lightning–

"I better dig in quick before Flynn and Fannie,
They'll have it all devoured and I won't get any!"

Mama laughed and then helped him jump up on top,
Where his paws sunk in– plop, plop, plop, plop.

The cheesecake was better than his favorite Smoked Gouda,
He pondered contently, like a little mouse Buddha.

The mouse family enjoyed a most pleasurable night,
Feasting together under the pale moonlight.

For cheesecake was a treat few mice had ever known,
It was far better than even a blueberry scone.

Though the Moon did not come in from the rain as they thought,
The truth of their discovery was more exciting than not.

CPSIA information can be obtained
at www.ICGtesting.com
Printed in the USA
LVIC06n0035110713
342353LV00002B